Alw

by David Ludwig

: This is a quick read summary based on the novel

"Always Hungry"

by David Ludwig

NOTE TO READERS:

This is a Summary & Analysis of Always Hungry by David Ludwig. You are encouraged to buy the full version.

TABLE OF CONTENTS

OVERVIEW

David Ludwig opens his book *Always Hungry: Conquer Cravings, Retrain Your Fat Cells, and Lose Weight Permanently* with testimonials from people who have taken part in his program during the pilot phase. The pilot phase of the program, Ludwig explains, was only 16 weeks long, while the program within the book is on a larger scale, taking months and becoming something that is more long term and permanent. Each person's testimonial describes their thoughts, feelings and emotions during and after this 16 week trial program. They talk about how the program, not only helped in their diet and weight loss goals, but how it helped improve their lifestyles, and enhanced their way of living.

After this portion of the book, Ludwig describes why some diets tend to fail and why we struggle so much with losing weight and even gaining weight on a long term scale. While we may lose the weight, it tends to only be temporarily, and it usually comes back. Ludwig states there is a way to lose the weight and keep it off permanently. He describes how many diets and weight loss plans look to deprivation, calorie counting and excessive work outs in order to lose this weight, but it always falls short of what we truly need to keep the weight off. These weight loss plans, he says, do not approach the real reason we struggle with weight. They only scratch the surface issue rather than scratching the core cause of weight gain.

He proceeds to talk about what we need to do in order to change that way of thinking and how when we begin to change our thinking when it comes to diet and weight loss, it becomes easier to lose that extra weight. He discusses how our bodies react to foods whether it is in a positive or negative way, and how that is actually what creates access body weight rather than having too many calories, or even too few calories. The problem with calorie counting and working out to burn the calories, we tend to not get enough calories to our bodies and it thinks it is starving. That in turn makes us feel like we are hungry and are in dire need of food. He states that our bodies already have a natural weight loss and weight gain system, that when we deprive the body of food, that system gets thrown out of whack.

Ludwig presents the problem that falls in the idea that in order to lose weight, you need to eat less. When you eat less, you deprive your body of calories and nutrients it needs. It begins to feel like it is starving and then hordes the calories it does have which in turn results in fat cells not sharing these vital nutrients and us gaining weight. When you provide your body with good foods the body doesn't become a hoarder and it becomes easier to lose weight as our body readjusts to maintain a healthy metabolism rate. He uses studies to show where his thoughts and ideas are stemming from as well as presents his own research and studies to show a foundation in his program, including an experiment that he conducted on himself before taking it to clinical trials.

David Ludwig places a lot of emphasis on the natural science of our bodies and how they act and react towards food, or lack of food. He discusses foods that one may think is healthy and provides a healthy alternative to something unhealthy, but in reality the alternative could be worse. He discusses the dangers of artificially flavored, processed and sugar filled foods and how the negative effects of these foods extend beyond our weight and into our general health and well being. He discusses how body fat is in fact critical to our health and well being rather than something to want to get rid of and change about ourselves. He discusses that the vitamins and nutrients our bodies need should not all be treated the same way. Some are good while some are bad. Just because something is a carbohydrate or fiber doesn't mean that it is automatically good for our bodies.

After presenting all the facts and what is wrong with different diets and weight loss plans, David Ludwig presents a solution to the problem. He theorizes that our focus needs to be on changing the way our fat cells react to food and how we can reprogram those in a good way as well as the way the brain reacts and perceives hunger. While many diet plans say to eat at a certain time and a certain amount, which may turn into depriving your body of things, this plan focuses its attention on eating when one is hungry and eating foods we love until we feel satisfied. The solution also focuses making healthier substitutes for foods that are damaging to our bodies and overall health. For example instead of reaching for a honey bun, reach for some nuts or fruit. The calorie amounts may be the same but the nutritional affects of the nuts/fruits are better than the honey bun we are craving, and the way the body reacts to both is significantly different. There is an underlying idea that we need to learn to listen to what our bodies need and don't need.

He stresses that the inability to lose weight is not a weakness or something to be ashamed of, as some parts of society would like us to think. He stresses in order to change our thinking about food and weight loss; we also need to change our thinking on the inability to lose weight. He makes suggestions on supplements and alternatives to incorporating the "good fat" into our diets and taking the "bad carbohydrates" out of our bodies. He also discusses the need to regulate the insulin the body naturally creates and how a disrupting in the creation of this product could have dire results and become diabetes and other diseases. Ludwig discusses how being overweight could put a person at a higher risk for a variety of diseases including heart attack and stroke.

David Ludwig mentions there are things one needs to do in order to prepare themselves to make such a life altering change. He proposes that his plan will address all the issues other diet and weight loss plans fail to address as well as solve them. He provides recipes that are convenient, delicious and satisfying as well as translating the latest insights to provide weight loss without being hungry and with the maximum possible benefits. He discusses how keeping track of our progress and how our bodies are reacting to the changes and how they react negatively if we happen to falter a little bit. He talks about the importance other factors in life such as sleep and stress levels have in our weight loss goals.

His plan begins with reducing the amount of certain foods we eat for 2 weeks as well as increasing activity levels. He discusses finding ways to motivate yourself and focusing on the reason you would want to make this major change in your life. He again stresses and emphasizes that obesity is not a weakness and something we can get a handle on and change. He admits we will be tempted, but states the plan is very simple to get back on track with and even allows for moments when we give into temptation. David Ludwig doesn't pretend to have all the answers; he simply states what he has found in his research of other studies as well as within his own studies. He also includes a lot of recipes that sound delicious and are easy to make that also have the ability to adapt to different dietary needs.

IMPORTANT PEOPLE

David Ludwig: David is the author of the book. He spent extensive about of time during his career researching and studying the effects of nutrition on the body and why obesity continues to be an epidemic within the country.

Participants: It is difficult to narrow down each of the testimonies into each individual person. Throughout the book David includes testimonies from people who participated in the initial pilot phase of the program. The testimonies include thoughts and emotions people felt while going through the program as well as the responses the received from those around them.

Barry Sears and Dr. Robert Atkins: These two are fellow diet authors whom David Ludwig incorporated into his nutritional and diet studies. Barry Sears wrote *The Zone Diet* and Dr.

Atkins is the creator of the Atkin's diet. David Ludwig was also inspired by the nutritional works of scientists like George Cahill and Jean Mayer.

CHAPTER SUMMARIES AND KEY POINTS

Testimonies:

Various people who took part in the pilot phase provide their experiences, thoughts and emotions through the trial. This section includes things people learned throughout the sixteen weeks they participated in the program. Every testimony included reflects what the program is designed to achieve. Something in common with all the testimonies is each person talks about how their notions about dieting and weight loss have changed, even how the viewpoints of the people around them have changed. People rave about how great they now feel because of the solution. Some even comment about the continued struggle with temptations and cravings.

Participants discuss how impressed they are with their results and how much they have learned through the process. Each testimony is accompanied with a first name, age, location, how much weight they lost and how much their waist decreased through the program. This helps gives readers an idea of what to expect as well as shows readers how results will vary and depend on the person. Everyone mentioned how their opinion on food has changed through the program and how their motivation and general self value increased because of Ludwig's program. The testimonies all feel authentic and not as if they were replicated.

Key Takeaways:

One may wonder what could be taken away from simple testimonies of people who participated in a pilot version of a weight loss solution. But, there are plenty of things to learn.

- Each person will have a different reaction to the program. No one is the same and will not have the same reaction as others.

- The solution is as much about gaining the self confidence and motivation as it is about learning about food and weight loss.

- Through the program our outlook on food will be different and the things that we crave will become different.

PROLOGUE

David Ludwig gives a brief overview of the issues that surround conventional diet and weight loss plans and what his plan "Always Hungry" strives to do for those who participate. He discusses what the program is designed to do and how participants can benefit from it. He also talks about how the participants in the first 16 week pilot benefited and results he discovered from this pilot phase. He gives a brief description of what readers will be able to find in the book including recipes and testimonials. He also provides contact information so readers can write to him about their own experiences. He wants to know how his solution has been helpful to others and what they have learned.

Key Takeaways:

· Calorie reduction ends in hunger, feeling deprived and fatigue. In the end we will succumb to temptations.

- Each body responds to the program differently. One cannot expect the same results that someone else had. Some many experience rapid weight loss, some will experience waist reduction, as well as reduced risk of other obesity related diseases.
- This is not a typical low carbohydrate diet. There are 3 phases to retrain the body and it's reactions of the foods we eat.

CHAPTER 1: THE BIG PICTURE

The author goes into detail about the common trends in dieting and previous thoughts on weight loss. He discusses how the body naturally alters our metabolism to reach an internally set weight point. That point can be manipulated. When we try to change behavior our body fights back, but when we change biology, the behavior will quickly follow. Ludwig began by doing food based experiments on himself with changes in his diet to see how his body reacted to changes such as reducing starches, increasing fats, even slightly increasing proteins. Ludwig mentions how important these changes are to the overall well being our bodies and minds. When we try to cut out something completely from our diet, the body begins to crave it which leads to binging on items that bring adverse reactions with it. We need to learn how to properly supply our body with the vitamins and nutrients it needs.

Many diets and weight loss plans focus on calories, and have the idea of eat less calories than we burn means we will lose weight. This kind of thinking is actually counter-productive because the body needs calories to function. All calories are not the same, calories in a piece of fruit is different than those in a bag of chips. We should not treat them as the same when it comes to weight loss. Many of these same weight loss and diet programs put a lot of blame on the person, stating they need discipline for the program to work and if they falter then they have no willpower or resolve. This is part of the thinking we need to change in order to be successful in weight loss goals. The issue is not about changing what we eat or how much we eat, but our outlook on how we eat and the items we choose to digest when craving something specific.

He begins talking about how our body's fat cells are more than just storage for extra calories. It is the master control of insulin. Ludwig emphasizes that we need to change the idea that overeating causes weight gain, but realize that weight gain is what causes overeating. When we deprive the body of calories, it goes into a sort of survival mode where it begins to store calories and triggers alarms that it needs calories i.e hunger. He discusses that weight gain is an issue of calorie balance and calories not being distributed to the body correctly, not an overabundance of calories as some other diets may have us believe. We need to forget the idea of counting and cutting calories in order to reduce weight, but regain a balance in how they are distributed through the body. Our bodies are more complex than we think, and not easily manipulated as one may imagine.

Key Takeaways:

- Eating less calories than the calories we burn is only setting ourselves up for failure. We need to learn what calories are good for us and which ones cause problems.

- Calorie abundance is not the issue, but calorie balance is. When we reduce the calories in our body, it goes into a survival mode and begins to hoard the calories it does have while other parts of our body does not get the calories needed to function.

- Plan is to eat until satisfied, not full. Tame fat by foods that lower insulin and redirect calories. Include a lifestyle of physical activity that we find enjoyable as well as getting enough sleep and finding effective ways to relieve stress.

CHAPTER 2: THE PROBLEM

The main problem with the conventional diet plans, according to David Ludwig, is that they focus on calories for weight loss. No one is able to accurately count calories and maintain a balance, who can honestly say how many calories are in eat item we each or how many calories are being burned while doing a specific physical activity. The idea of needing lower fat has caused food companies to turn to alternative carbohydrates which in turn have cause more adverse affects than unprocessed foods. It has become more popular to accommodate cravings with processed foods rather than whole, natural foods. Natural health foods like nuts and avocado have gained bad reputations for being high in fat, but that fat is a good kind we need to consume. Modern sedentary lifestyles also play a part in weight gain as we are not as active as we once were about 20 years ago. Studies have shown it is easier to gain calories than it is to get rid of them.

Genetics may also play a part in our weight gaining issues. Sometimes someone with relatives who struggle with weight, will struggle with their weight as well. Some people tend to have a gene that creates a certain hormone that tells the body when enough fat has been consumed, others do not have this gene, which makes the body feel like it is constantly starving. Delicious tasting foods also play a role in weight gain as they over stimulate the brain's pleasure circuits. Over time we teach our bodies to find pleasure in processed, highly sugared foods rather than finding pleasure in something more natural. Food industry capitalizes on the three major flavors: salty, sweet, and fatty. Excessive exposure to certain flavors triggers a pleasure censor and become a reward of sorts for the body. Ludwig explains we are able to train our taste buds to find pleasure or displeasure in different flavors.

Many people would like to think that excessive weight gain and overeating are a result of low willpower and the inability to control oneself when it comes to eating. Research has found no correlation being weight and a person's inner qualities. Everyone has difficulties with weight loss or even weight gain; while some struggle to lose weight; others also have a difficult time gaining weight. Everyone's body is different and responds differently to certain stimuli. Willpower, genetics, tastiness of foods and physical activity all have influences on weight, but they are not the underlying cause to weight gain or weight loss. Obesity can lead to other health related issues such as diabetes, heart attack, or kidney failure. Many take a variety of medications for blood pressure, blood sugar, cholesterol in hopes of staving off some of these issues. Obesity in childhood could lead to obesity and other struggles later in life.

Key Takeaways:

- Calories are not the underlying cause of weight gain. We need to pay attention to the ingredients in the foods we buy and think about processed foods over fresh foods and how they related to our bodies.

- There are many factors that play a role in weight such as genetics, physical activity, the taste of foods, and overall will power. We need to take a look how each of those factors could also play a role in our individual body's results in weight loss.

- Obesity is an epidemic that can lead to other more serious illness later in life. Diabetes, heart attack, stroke and kidney failure are all issues that could be related to obesity. Medications can only do so much when it comes to preventing these issues.

CHAPTER 3: THE SCIENCE

Common thinking of body weight and weight loss has been calorie intake minus calorie expenditure equals calories stored (or fat stored). It is the idea that the food we consume has more calories than we burn meaning fat is what is being stored. This only leads to the idea that if there is too much fat then the solution is to eat less and exercise more. In many studies those who have lost weight in weight loss programs end up gaining it back over time. The problem is not the inability to count calories or self control, but in the misunderstanding of what really causes obesity. One problem with counting calories is that it gives the illusion of having control, but cutting calories from our diet only launches a counter measure within our body. Meaning our bodies fight back; and the more we lose the more we force our bodies to fight back.

When we under-eat the body burns less calories which makes us want to cut more calories because we aren't seeing the desired effect. We end up thinking we are not doing enough or cutting enough calories. But in reality, the body works in the opposite way, when we consume MORE calories we burn more because it speeds up our metabolism. Calories are what fuels our bodies, when we cut calories, our bodies do not have the fuel needed to function. Because the body has its own weight management system it is difficult to make a change in either direction. Body fat plays a significant role in health and long life. Fat protects the internal organs and protects us from the cold. Fat is the fuel tank for our body. Our entire body requires a lot of calories just to function, when there is a significant reduction in those calories, our bodies cannot function properly and can result in loss of consciousness, seizure, coma or even death. Our energy comes from carbohydrates, protein, and fat are stored differently.

Body substances combined with diet are what effect fat cell behavior, one of the main substance that effect fat cell behavior is insulin. Diabetes is caused by problems with the functions and production of insulin which helps control the calorie flow throughout the body. Too much insulin drives fat cells to increase which causes weight gain. Less insulin production causes the fat cells to decrease and causes weight loss. Some of the foods we eat, packaged foods, lead to too much insulin being produced, therefore causing the fat cells to increase. Overeating does not produce fat cell growth; fat cell growth produces overeating. When fat cells grow, they tend to hold onto the calories being stored and do not allow for proper distribution to the rest of the body. Low calorie diets mean the calories needed for the body to function are lower which causes the brain to panic and sends out an alarm demanding more food.

When our bodies go into a panicked state, the fat cells begin to hoard calories, not sharing them with the rest of the body.

This becomes a never ending battle with our bodies as we continue to eat more food, but endlessly feel hungry because the fat cells are keeping the calories to themselves. When we increase the fat storage with a low quality diet the fat cells expand, and when they reach capacity they send out a distress call and the immune system responds. Body fat and the immune system are linked together, each helping the other out. This link is disrupted in obesity, and our bodies essentially begin to fight itself trying to find the intruding element. When the immune system struggles to fight, it calls for help from cells in order areas of the body, leaving us susceptible to inflammation.

Key Takeaways:

- Weight and fat cells are related to one another. The fat cells store calories needed for the body to function. When there are too few calories, fat cells hoard calories which causes weight gain.

- Body fat is important to maintain health and a long life. It protects all the internal organs from harm and protects our entire body from the effects of coldness.

- When calories needed to fuel the body are lowered significantly the body begins to feel like it is starving and goes into survival mode, seeking out calories in any form it can find. This is when we cave and binge on unhealthy foods.

- Insulin is a major factor in weight as it is controls how and where fuel is distributed throughout the body. Too much causes the fat cells to increase dramatically.

- When the fat cells are in distress, the immune system responds and can begin to attack the body as the system seeks out what is causing the cells distress.

CHAPTER 4: THE SOLUTION

When the body begins to fight back, hunger and craving begin to raise in turn causing metabolism to slow down. The metabolism slows because the body does not want to burn the few calories it has to function. An effective approach to weight loss would be to seek out foods that lower insulin rather than lowering calories. Reducing insulin allows the fat cells to release its calorie storage and hunger subsides, cravings lessen and weight loss can occur naturally. Decreasing carbohydrates is an effective way to lower insulin. Increasing protein can create more glucagon which can counteract insulin, lower its effects on the body. We should be seeking out healthy fats from sources like olive oil and nuts to help fuel the body for hours.

Just as all calories are different, all carbohydrates are different. How the foods affect the body differ from food to food which forms the glycemic index, whereas the glycemic load accounts for carbohydrate foods. Fat has always been seen with a negative reputation and fat substitutes have become popular, but are worse for our bodies than the natural fats. These substitutes fill our bodies with processed materials that digest quickly and cause us to feel hungry quicker. Also like calories and carbohydrates, not all fats should be treated the same. Certain fats are good for our diets, while others only make matters worse. Supplements such as fish oil and flax oil can help add to these healthy fats. These oils and other supplements help the body gain the things it needs when the foods we eat do not provide them.

Our digestive tracks contain bacteria, viruses, and other micro-organisms which are beneficial to the function of our bodies. They all play a role in maintaining health and are again different for each person. Good bacteria reside in certain foods like yogurt. Sugars also play a small role in health, but it is not the amount of sugars in our bodies, but how it gets absorbed into the body that makes a different.

Sugar substitutes are often added to foods, along with salt which can also have adverse effects. Highly processed foods do not contain the vitamins, minerals, probiotics and other qualities that are essential to healthy bodily functions. They are full of preservatives, additives, and artificial flavoring. The idea for the "Always Hungry Solution" is to turn our diets back to things that are natural rather than things that are pre-processed and altered.

Key Takeaways:

- Decreasing carbohydrates and increasing protein can help in reducing the production of insulin. This will in turn help with weight loss as insulin does not become over produced in the body.

- There are good and bad calories, fats, sugars, carbohydrates, and other vitamins/minerals. We cannot treat all of them the same and need to understand how each plays a role in our bodily functions.

- Highly processed foods have more ingredients in them that cause us more harm than the natural foods they replace. We need to begin to shift from eating processed foods to eating things that are fresh.

CHAPTER 5: PREPARING TO CHANGE YOUR LIFE

The"Always Hungry" plan has the purpose of addresses the causes of weight gain whereas typical low fat diets do not address these concerns. Typical low fat diets seek to reduce calorie intake which does not address the causes of weight gain but induces it. The "Always Hungry Solution" aims to be different in that it is designed to decrease insulin levels and reprogram fat cells. It aims to decrease hunger and cravings while speeding up metabolism which will then result in natural weight loss. There are three phases to the program which are 1) conquering cravings, 2) plan to retrain fat cells, 3) customizing a diet for your body's specific needs. The solution is supposed to be something that can be turned into a long term solution rather than something temporarily.

There are recipes included in the plan are designed to teach about new insights to weight loss with the maximum benefit, they are convenient and simply to make in under 30 minutes, they also are delicious, satisfying and are suitable for all diets including those that are vegetarian and gluten free. Ludwig claims that following this plan the participant will find that their cravings will become cravings for something healthier. The plan is expected to help people feel better, and to increase energy levels. The plan is designed to not only change a person's outlook on food and body weight, but also helps change their opinion of body image. The recipes included are designed to make the fat cells share the calories it has rather than hording them.

Before starting the plan, one needs to prepare them and discover their motivation for making this major life change. David Ludwig asks readers/participants to take seven days to mentally prepare for this challenge. During those seven days we are to figure out how to track the progress made, figure out what will work for the preparation phase for the foods (either the night before or that day), find a way to get organized (make things easy to find), and figure out how to forget all previous notions about calories. Readers are asked to keep track of hunger, cravings, energy level, sleep patterns, even their mood for each day. It is also during this time one will need to take pre-plan data like weight and waist measurements.

During the seven day preparation, readers are supposed to purge their kitchen of all unhealthy temptations and begin their shopping lists for the upcoming week or two weeks. When there is temptation present it is easier to fall off the plan, so it is best to get rid of anything that is tempting. They are also asked to make a long term motivation plan, what do you hope to accomplish in the long-run aside from simply losing a few extra pounds. If short term goals are made, once they are completed we are tempted to quit the program, where as if something long term is planned there is more motivation to continue longer. This plan is designed to be a permanent change rather than a quick fix.

Key Takeaways:

- Before beginning the program, one needs to understand the purpose of the program and what each phase is design to accomplish.
- Take seven days prior to beginning the plan to prepare yourself mentally and organize your goals and tracking system. Being organized will help in keeping with the program
- Before beginning the program purge kitchen of everything that is unhealthy and prepare a list of

healthy foods for the coming weeks. Also prepare bedroom for a peaceful night's rest, romance and reading. Nothing else (meaning no television, computers or other distractions).

CHAPTER 6: PHASE 1: CONQUERING CRAVINGS

The idea to curb the cravings is to start by replacing fast digesting carbohydrates with slow digesting ones that can be found in vegetables, fruits, and legumes. On a standard diet, some people can develop an insulin resistance and inflammation, this plan is designed to reverse that occurrence. It is okay to eat whenever you feel hungry, but eat until you reach a point of satisfaction, not a point of feeling overly full. This allows the body to move out of the starvation mode. Remember to drink plenty of water as opposed to sugary drinks, also develop a sleep routine that will allow your body to get enough sleep at night and learn positive ways to relieve stress such as yoga or meditation.

In addition to reducing the amount of fast digesting carbohydrates in your diet, begin adding in a 15 minute after dinner walk. This will allow you to have a chance to reconnect with your neighborhood, pet, loved ones and yourself. This small amount of activity will also help with the digestion process. This could be a great moment for mediation and reflection on the day. Your bedroom should already be prepared for a good night sleep, now you will need to honor a bedtime meaning once it hits that bed time put away the phones, computers, turning off the television, and allow your body to unwind and relax. This will help keep stress levels down and makes it easier to make positive changes in your life.

As part of your bedtime ritual add in a moment of stress relief such as bedtime yoga (there is a difference between bedtime yoga and other forms of yoga), mediation, or journaling. Take time to reflect on your reasons for making this change. Ludwig states soon people would begin to feel more energy; the brain will begin to recognize that it has enough fuel for the day. Your need for outside calories lowers and you will stay fuller for a longer period of time. Ludwig stresses everyone's body is different and will react differently to the plan. Make portion sizes whatever is right for you to feel satisfied. Each meal is flexible and can adapt for any moderation.

Key Takeaways:

- Curb cravings by replacing fast digesting carbohydrates with slow digesting carbohydrates. Instead of reaching for the glazed donut, grab an orange or apple, you will feel fuller longer and get many essential vitamins and minerals.

- Begin a short walk after dinner to help with digestion. Find ways to meditation and positively reduce stress levels. Make sure your bedroom is conducive to a restful night sleep without distractions.

- Remember to keep track of your progress, moods, any changes you notice in energy, sleep pattern and stress levels. Also keep in mind every one reacts differently to the suggested changes.

CHAPTER 7: PHASE 2: RETRAINING YOUR FAT CELLS

After two weeks in phase one, it is time to move on to phase two. Participants should have begun to notices changes. The length of phase two depends on the person; it could be a month to 6 months or longer. In this phase participants will begin to introduce more foods with carbohydrates in them, but the slow digesting kind, and Ludwig provides a list and charts of appropriate choices. The goal of this phase is now to sustain the weight and maintain a healthy lifestyle and diet. The weight will continue to slowly come off as the body continues to readjust to the changes. Again the process is different depending on the person.

At this point, participants will also be adding more physical activity by adding in something enjoyable like swimming, biking, playing a sport or dancing; anything that provides mobility in a lifestyle that is centered on sedentary work.

Those in the program will find they have more energy and want to be moving rather than being stationary. Sleep should have become more restful which helps fine tune the body's metabolism and provides a safeguard to your health. Along with more motion, this phase adds more stress relief (which could also be the physical activity).

Emphasis is place on keeping track of the progress being made. There will be times when we cave in to temptation; those moments should be recorded as well to notice how our bodies react negatively to foods we once craved. Keeping track of our progress makes it easier to understand how our individual bodies work and help us learn how to listen to what our bodies need. The plan is designed so that it is easy to get back on track after a slip. Every moment throughout the process is a learning moment, so remember not to blame yourself or quit. Use it as motivation to get back on track.

Key Takeaways:

- The length of phase two depends on the person; certain foods are being re-introduced into the diet. Weight may plateau for a period and that is okay.

- Physical activity and stress relief are also increased in this phase to help the body react to not only foods ingested but also outside stimulants.

- Keeping track of progress is an important learning tool. In order to make progress one needs to learn how their body works and what it needs. Keeping track allows for this learning to happen.

CHAPTER 8: PHASE 3: LOSE WEIGHT PERMANENTLY

After a period of time determine by you, there should be a considerable amount of weight lose, waist reduction, and overall better well being. This is the point in the program where participants tailor the diet and other elements to their specific needs. This allows you to maintain everything permanently, not just temporarily. More processed carbohydrates like bread are re-introduced into the diet, but in moderation. Through the other phases you are reconnecting with your body and providing what it needs to function properly, this phase is where you take everything you have learn over the course of the program and tailor it to fit your preferences.

Personalizing your plan in phase three is not only for your diet but also for your sleep pattern, daily stress relief and physical activity. This phase is to ensure that your new healthy lifestyle is one you can enjoy long term. You can go to restaurant and be able to order something you will enjoy, but remain in your diet without causing adverse reactions. This point you may also find yourself looking for ways to be more mobile such as parking farther away from the building to walk more or taking the stairs instead of the elevator. Sleep will comes easier because of the increased movement and stress relief, your body will naturally feel relaxed rather than tense.

This a point in your life change that you can look back at your beginning life change and re-evaluate it. Is the reason for a healthier lifestyle the same? If not discover a new one. If it is then continue on the path to success and strive for that goal. Ludwig suggests participants to continue using the tools they used in the first two phase and continue to keep track of progress and motivations as well as moments when temptation wins. Ludwig also provides ideas to turn leftovers into delicious meals the next day.

Key Takeaways:

- After completing phase one and two, it is time to customize and design a plan that suits your own individual needs and preferences. This is where you make the plan permanent and maintain a healthy weight and diet.

- Continuing to maintain a daily log of your progress, moods, reactions, sleep and stress are essential to the program as it will help you keep your motivation as the forefront of your mind.

- Experiment with recipes and reinvent leftovers into a new meal the next day. The plan shouldn't be something difficult or something to dread, but something that is fun and exciting.

CHAPTER 9: RECIPES

This chapter is full of different recipes you can use throughout the "Always Hungry Solution." There is something for every meal of the day including a few snacks. It is easy to adapt the recipes to dietary needs such as lactose free, gluten free, and vegetarian. Ludwig provides a list of suggested substitutes, for example if you are a vegetarian he provides substitutes for chicken that will provide the same effects. Drinks are also included such as a power protein shake.

Each recipe includes serving size, preparation time, cook time, easy to follow directions, ingredients, tips and suggestions, and nutritional values (calories, proteins, carbohydrates etc). With each recipe name, it lets you know which phase the recipe is suitable for, and you can continue using phase 1 and 2 recipes into phase 3. There are no recipes that take longer than half an hour to cook. They are all simple to follow and to the point. There is nothing extravagant that would require a cooking device that can only be found in a restaurant. Basically, the recipes are basic and even the most novice of cooks could master these recipes.

The recipes take some of the best comfort foods and make them into a food that fits into the healthier diet such as sloppy joes (vegetarian version uses tofu instead of beef). Just reading the ingredients will make your mouth water. There are so many different flavor combinations that it makes it seem easy to be able to substitute or curb cravings with items out of this book.

Key Takeaways:

- Recipes are full of flavor and easy to adapt to any special dietary needs. They even include tips on what you can substitute to adapt them to your needs.

- Recipes are easy to follow and do not take more than half an hour to cook. Nor do they require any equipment that is not already in your kitchen.

EPILOGUE: ENDING THE MADNESS

Ludwig looks at healthy food as a case of national security. In ancient times the invading army would attack their enemy by poisoning food and water supplies. Ludwig suggests readers think of an invading army as attacking us by undermining our diets so we succumb to diseases like diabetes. He creates a scenario that is both frightening and an eye opener. He suggests we are a culture that condones processed foods full of artificial flavors and additives. He comments on the convenient accessibility of junk foods whereas whole foods are expensive and not as easily accessible. He mentions how society needs to take one a shared responsibility for public health rather than expecting it to fall onto the individual.

He provides a ten point plan to make healthy food a priority of national security. He interjects his belief that the government should regulate the food industry to regulate the market towards a healthier society. He continues to add in testimonies for people who have already participated in the program and their reactions to things they have learned about themselves as well as society. After this section of the book is the appendix which includes all the spreadsheets and data collection forms Ludwig suggests readers utilize while they are participating in the "Always Hungry Solution." This also includes a guide to cooking vegetables, whole grains, nuts and even seeds. Some of these items might be difficult to prepare, having this guide is essential.

Key Takeaways:

- We are responsible for the health and diet. We cannot expect someone else to do it for us.
- We are a culture that is focused on convenience, temporary fixes that are fast and easy to find.
- We are a culture focused on "junk" foods rather than naturally flavored foods.

A READER'S PERSPECTIVE

Always Hungry: Conquer Cravings, Retrain Your Fat Cells, and Lose Weight Permanently By David Ludwig is an interesting look on weight loss and how we have perceived it all wrong for countless years. He delves in the science behind what causes individuals to gain weight and struggle with losing it. The testimonials show what motivated other people and give readers a clear idea of how the plan is supposed to work, and has real people speaking volumes about it. Ludwig shares the fruits of his extensive research and studies to provide us with a concise diet and weight loss plan that works with our bodies rather than against it. He not only provides a solution to the problem, but he also tries to come up with a cause of the problem.

What David Ludwig does is highlight the journey of self discovery and weight loss through understanding how food and our bodies respond to one another. He does a great job at showing how intricate and complex the body is and the dangers of that system being out of sync. Everything within our bodies are interrelated and what we put into our bodies also play a part into that relationship. David provides a lot of scientific research and foundation as the basis for his "Always Hungry Solution," he even performs his own experiments to discover everything he mentions in this book. Ludwig weaves in testimonials from people who have already been through the program. These are real people with real experiences and emotions. This helps the reader to relate to the program and have the confidence to keep with it for a long term commitment. He outlines key points where we might struggle with adhering to a specific diet or plan.

David Ludwig is able to take a magnitude of scientific terminology and research and puts it all into terms that everyone can understand. There are many things in this book that I would not have understood, but he puts it into a language that is simplistic. This book is easy to follow and easy to come back to after leaving off. The program Ludwig suggests is not one with a lot of steps or sacrifices, if anything it adds to things you are already doing and enhances your life. One thing about this book is that Ludwig mentions modern diet and weight loss plans, but he does not name them specifically nor does he downplay what other plans have accomplished. It shows his respect for his peers and contemporaries, while he offers a different alternative to their plans.

The recipes Ludwig created are easy to follow and simple to create. Each of the recipes takes about 30 minutes or less to cook, meaning a person does not have to spend countless hours trying to cook a gourmet meal that they may not enjoy. The preparation time is about the same or less, and many of the recipes can be prepared a day or two ahead of time. Each recipe has ingredients that are easy to find in any grocery store and utilizes common kitchen supplies. Ludwig's recipes are a combination of flavors that will appeal to any and all taste buds. He talks about taste and flavor playing a part in weight gain as we eat foods we find pleasurable. These recipes bring out those pleasure censors to help curve cravings towards something healthier.

While many of the things Ludwig mentions throughout his book may seem repetive or like something readers have heard elsewhere, Ludwig presents it in a new way. He presents the same information in a way that is easy to adapt to the reader's personal lifestyle and makes the process seem incredibly easy. Throughout the book, he also stresses that everyone's body will respond to the "Always Hungry Solution" differently and to not get discouraged if you are not getting the exact same results as someone else may have. He puts a lot of emphasis on individuality of the plan and how easy it is to adapt the plan your needs and life, whereas other books want participants to be doing the exact same thing as the next person.

AUTHOR'S STYLE

Although Ludwig's work is solid and grounded in extensive research, analysis and studies, he presents his findings in a straight forward way making his weight loss and health principles easy to understand and grasp. He does not overwhelm readers with intense information and instruction. He presents his findings and solutions in a clear and concise way that makes readers want to read the book again, and recommend it to others. He allows for the reader to take a break from the science and research information with testimonies from those who have already participated. This shows he doesn't want to overwhelm his readers but provide a clear understanding of what they will be undertaking if they decide to try his program. The testimonies bring his research and theories to life and memorable for the readers.

He outlines each chapter with a new idea and understanding of the weight loss and nutrition field. He elaborates on ideas found in various studies performed throughout the years, his own extensive research into the epidemic of obesity, and a solution to solve this problem on a personal level. He maintains a tone of empathy and understanding. He wants to empower his readers to make the step towards a healthy life rather than shaming them into taking that step. Repeatedly throughout the book he emphasizes individuality and how each body reacts differently to different stimuli. He wants his readers to understand what works for one person may not work for another. He maintains this idea and tone throughout the book until the very end, never once does he deviate from this theme. *Always Hungry: Conquer Cravings, Retrain Your Fat Cells, and Lose Weight Permanently* is a book that is focused on busting the myths and misconceptions revolving around weight loss and providing a sensible alternative to depriving your body of essential nutrients.

Made in the USA
Coppell, TX
13 February 2020

15799068R00036